Seneca the Younger
Apocolocyntosis

ERIS
gems

I WISH TO PLACE ON RECORD THE
proceedings in heaven October 13 last, of
the new year which begins this auspicious
age. It shall be done without malice or
favour. This is the truth. Ask if you like how
I know it? To begin with, I am not bound to
please you with my answer. Who will com-
pel me? I know the same day made me free,
which was the last day for him who made
the proverb true—One must be born either
a Pharaoh or a fool. If I choose to answer, I
will say whatever trips off my tongue. Who
has ever made the historian produce witness to swear for him? But if an authority must be produced, ask of the man who
saw Drusilla translated to heaven: the same
man will aver he saw Claudius on the road,
dot and carry one. Will he nill he, all that
happens in heaven he needs must see. He
is the custodian of the Appian Way; by that
route, you know, both Tiberius and Augustus went up to the gods. Question him, he
will tell you the tale when you are alone;
before company he is dumb. You see he

3

swore in the Senate that he beheld Drusilla mounting heavenwards, and all he got for his good news was that everybody gave him the lie: since when he solemnly swears he will never bear witness again to what he has seen, not even if he had seen a man murdered in open market. What he told me I report plain and clear, as I hope for his health and happiness.

Now had the sun with shorter course
drawn in his risen light,
And by equivalent degrees grew the
dark hours of night:
Victorious Cynthia now held sway
over a wider space,
Grim winter drove rich autumn out,
and now usurped his place;
And now the fiat had gone forth that
Bacchus must grow old,
The few last clusters of the vine were
gathered ere the cold:

I shall make myself better understood, if I

say the month was October, the day was the
thirteenth. What hour it was I cannot certainly tell; philosophers will agree more of-
ten than clocks; but it was between midday
and one after noon. "Clumsy creature!" you
say. "The poets are not content to describe
sunrise and sunset, and now they even dis-
turb the midday siesta. Will you thus ne-
glect so good an hour?"

> Now the sun's chariot had gone by the
> middle of his way;
> Half wearily he shook the reins, near-
> er to night than day,
> And led the light along the slope that
> down before him lay.

Claudius began to breathe his last, and
could not make an end of the matter.
Then Mercury, who had always been much
pleased with his wit, drew aside one of the
three Fates, and said: "Cruel beldame, why
do you let the poor wretch be tormented?
After all this torture cannot he have a rest?

Four and sixty years it is now since he began to pant for breath. What grudge is this you bear against him and the whole empire? Do let the astrologers tell the truth for once; since he became emperor, they have never let a year pass, never a month, without laying him out for his burial. Yet it is no wonder if they are wrong, and no one knows his hour. Nobody ever believed he was really quite born. Do what has to be done: Kill him, and let a better man rule in empty court".

Clotho replied: "Upon my word, I did wish to give him another hour or two, until he should make Roman citizens of the half dozen who are still outsiders. (He made up his mind, you know, to see the whole world in the toga, Greeks, Gauls, Spaniards, Britons, and all.) But since it is your pleasure to leave a few foreigners for seed, and since you command me, so be it". She opened her box and out came three spindles. One was for Augurinus, one for Baba, one for Claudius. "These three", she says, "I will cause to die within one year and at no great distance apart, and I will not dismiss him unattended. Think of all the thousands of men he was wont to see following after him, thousands going before, thousands all crowding about him, and it would never do to leave him alone on a sudden. These boon companions will satisfy him for the nonce".

This said, she twists the thread
around his ugly spindle once,
Snaps off the last bit of the life of that
Imperial dunce.
But Lachesis, her hair adorned, her
tresses neatly bound,
Pierian laurel on her locks, her brows
with garlands crowned,
Plucks me from out the snowy wool
new threads as white as snow,
Which handled with a happy touch
change colour as they go,
Not common wool, but golden wire;
the Sisters wondering gaze,

As age by age the pretty thread runs
down the golden days.
World without end they spin away, the
happy fleeces pull;
What joy they take to fill their hands
with that delightful wool!
Indeed, the task performs itself: no
toil the spinners know:
Down drops the soft and silken thread
as round the spindles go;
Fewer than these are Tithon's years,
not Nestor's life so long.
Phoebus is present: glad he is to sing
a merry song;
Now helps the work, now full of hope
upon the harp doth play;
The Sisters listen to the song that
charms their toil away.
They praise their brother's melodies,
and still the spindles run,
Till more than man's allotted span the
busy hands have spun.
Then Phoebus says, "O sister Fates! I
pray take none away,

But suffer this one life to be longer
than mortal day.
Like me in face and lovely grace, like
me in voice and song,
He'll bid the laws at length speak out
that have been dumb so long,
Will give unto the weary world years
prosperous and bright.
Like as the daystar from on high scat-
ters the stars of night,
As, when the stars return again, clear
Hesper brings his light,
Or as the ruddy dawn drives out the
dark, and brings the day,
As the bright sun looks on the world,
and speeds along its way
His rising car from morning's gates:
so Caesar doth arise,
So Nero shows his face to Rome be-
fore the people's eyes,
His bright and shining countenance
illumines all the air,
While down upon his graceful neck
fall rippling waves of hair".

Thus Apollo. But Lachesis, quite as ready to cast a favourable eye on a handsome man, spins away by the handful, and bestows years and years upon Nero out of her own pocket. As for Claudius, they tell everybody

to speed him on his way
With cries of joy and solemn litany.

At once he bubbled up the ghost, and there was an end to that shadow of a life. He was listening to a troupe of comedians when he died, so you see I have reason to fear those gentry. The last words he was heard to speak in this world were these. When he had made a great noise with that end of him which talked easiest, he cried out, "Oh dear, oh dear! I think I have made a mess of myself". Whether he did or no, I cannot say, but certain it is he always did make a mess of everything.

What happened next on earth it is mere

waste of time to tell, for you know it all well enough, and there is no fear of your ever forgetting the impression which that public rejoicing made on your memory. No one forgets his own happiness. What happened in heaven you shall hear: for proof please apply to my informant. Word comes to Jupiter that a stranger had arrived, a man well set up, pretty grey; he seemed to be threatening something, for he wagged his head ceaselessly; he dragged the right foot. They asked him what nation he was of; he answered something in a confused mumbling voice: his language they did not understand. He was no Greek and no Roman, nor of any known race. On this Jupiter bids Hercules go and find out what country he comes from; you see Hercules had travelled over the whole world, and might be expected to know all the nations in it. But Hercules, the first glimpse he got, was really much taken aback, although not all the monsters in the world could frighten him; when he saw this new kind of object, with its extraordinary gait, and the voice of no terrestrial beast, but such as you might hear in the leviathans of the deep, hoarse and inarticulate, he thought his thirteenth labour had come upon him. When he looked closer, the thing seemed to be a kind of man. Up he goes, then, and says what your Greek finds readiest to his tongue:

"Who art thou, and what thy people?
Who thy parents, where thy home?"

Claudius was delighted to find literary men up there, and began to hope there might be some corner for his own historical works. So he caps him with another Homeric verse, explaining that he was Caesar:

"Breezes wafted me from Ilion unto the Ciconian land".

But the next verse was more true, and no less Homeric:

"Thither come, I sacked a city, slew
the people every one".

He would have taken in poor simple Hercules, but that Our Lady of Malaria was
there, who left her temple and came alone
with him: all the other gods he had left at
Rome. Quoth she, "The fellow's tale is nothing but lies. I have lived with him all these
years, and I tell you, he was born at Lyons.
You behold a fellow-burgess of Marcus. As I
say, he was born at the sixteenth milestone
from Vienne, a native Gaul. So of course he
took Rome, as a good Gaul ought to do. I
pledge you my word that in Lyons he was
born, where Licinus was king so many
years. But you that have trudged over more
roads than any muleteer that plies for hire,
you must have come across the people of
Lyons, and you must know that it is a far
cry from Xanthus to the Rhone". At this
point Claudius flared up, and expressed
his wrath with as big a growl as he could
manage. What he said nobody understood;

as a matter of fact, he was ordering my lady of Fever to be taken away, and making that sign with his trembling hand (which was always steady enough for that, if for nothing else) by which he used to decapitate men. He had ordered her head to be chopped off. For all the notice the others took of him, they might have been his own freedmen.

Then Hercules said, "You just listen to me, and stop playing the fool. You have come to the place where the mice nibble iron. Out with the truth, and look sharp, or I'll knock your quips and quiddities out of you". Then to make himself all the more awful, he strikes an attitude and proceeds in his most tragic vein:

"Declare with speed what spot you claim by birth.
Or with this club fall stricken to the earth!
This club hath oft times slaughtered haughty kings!

Why mumble unintelligible things?
What land, what tribe produced that
shaking head?
Declare it! On my journey when I sped
Far to the Kingdom of the triple King,
And from the Main Hesperian did
bring
The goodly cattle to the Argive town,
There I beheld a mountain looking
down
Upon two rivers: this the Sun espies
Right opposite each day he doth arise.
Hence, mighty Rhone, thy rapid tor-
rents flow,
And Arar, much in doubt which way
to go,
Ripples along the banks with shallow
roll.
Say, is this land the nurse that bred
thy soul?"

These lines he delivered with much spirit
and a bold front. All the same, he was not
quite master of his wits, and had some fear

of a blow from the fool. Claudius, seeing a mighty man before him, saw things looked serious and understood that here he had not quite the same pre-eminence as at Rome, where no one was his equal: the Gallic cock was worth most on his own dunghill. So this is what he was thought to say, as far as could be made out: "I did hope, Hercules, bravest of all the gods, that you would take my part with the rest, and if I should need a voucher, I meant to name you who know me so well. Do but call it to mind, how it was I used to sit in judgment before your temple whole days together during July and August. You know what miseries I endured there, in hearing the lawyers plead day and night. If you had fallen amongst these, you may think yourself very strong, but you would have found it worse than the sewers of Augeas: I drained out more filth than you did. But since I want..."

[Some pages have fallen out, in which Hercules must have been persuaded. The gods are now discussing what Hercules tells them.]

"No wonder you have forced your way into the Senate House: no bars or bolts can hold against you. Only do say what species of god you want the fellow to be made. An Epicurean god he cannot be: for they have no troubles and cause none. A Stoic, then? How can he be globular, as Varro says, without a head or any other projection? There is in him something of the Stoic god, as I can see now: he has neither heart nor head. Upon my word, if he had asked this boon from Saturn, he would not have got it, though he kept up Saturn's feast all the year round, a truly Saturnalian prince. A likely thing he will get it from Jove, whom he condemned for incest as far as in him lay: for he killed his son-in-law Silanus, because Silanus had a sister, a most charming girl, called Venus by all the world, and he preferred to call her Juno. Why, says he, I want to know why, his own sister? Read your books, stupid: you may go half-way at Athens, the whole way at Alexandria. Because the mice lick meal at Rome, you say. Is this creature to mend our crooked ways? What goes on in his own closet he knows not; and now he searches the regions of the sky, wants to be a god. Is it not enough that he has a temple in Britain, that savages worship him and pray to him as a god, so that they may find a fool to have mercy upon them?"

At last it came into Jove's head, that while strangers were in the House it was not lawful to speak or debate. "My lords and gentlemen", said he, "I gave you leave to ask questions, and you have made a regular farmyard of the place. Be so good as to keep the rules of the House. What will this person think of us, whoever he is?" So Claudius was led out, and the first to be asked his opinion was Father Janus: he had been made consul elect for the afternoon of the next first of July, being as shrewd a man as you could find on a summer's day: for he could see, as they say, before and behind. He made an eloquent harangue, because his life was passed in the forum, but too fast for the notary to take down. That is why I give no full report of it, for I don't want to change the words he used. He said a great deal of the majesty of the gods, and how the honour ought not to be given away to every Tom, Dick, or Harry. "Once", said he, "it was a great thing to become a god; now you have made it a farce. Therefore, that you may not think I am speaking against one person instead of the general custom, I propose that from this day forward the godhead be given to none of those who eat the fruits of the earth, or whom mother earth doth nourish. After this bill has been read a third time, whosoever is made, said, or portrayed to be god, I vote he be delivered over to the bogies, and at the next public show be flogged with a birch amongst the new gladiators". The next to be asked was Diespiter, son of Vica Pota, he also being consul elect, and a moneylender; by this trade he made a living, used to sell rights of citizenship in a small way. Hercules trips me up to him daintily, and tweaks him by the ear. So he uttered his opinion in these words: "Inasmuch as the blessed Claudius is akin to the blessed Augustus, and also to the blessed Augusta, his grandmother, whom he ordered to be made a goddess, and whereas he far surpasses all mortal men in wisdom, and seeing that it is for the public good that there be some one able to join Romulus in devouring boiled turnips, I propose that from this day forth blessed Claudius be a god, to enjoy that honour with all its appurtenances in as full a degree as any other before him, and that a note to that effect be added to Ovid's Metamorphoses". The meeting was divided, and it looked as though Claudius was to win the day. For Hercules saw his iron was in the fire, trotted here and trotted there, saying, "Don't deny me; I make a point of the matter. I'll do as much for you again, when you like; you roll my log, and I'll roll yours: one hand washes another".

Then arose the blessed Augustus, when his turn came, and spoke with much eloquence. "I call you to witness, my lords and gentlemen", said he, "that since the day I was made a god I have never uttered one word. I always mind my own business. But now I can keep on the mask no longer, nor conceal the sorrow which shame makes all the greater. Is it for this I have made peace by land and sea? For this have I calmed intestine wars? For this, laid a firm foundation of law for Rome, adorned it with buildings, and all that—my lords, words fail me; there are none can rise to the height of my indignation. I must borrow that saying of the eloquent Messala Corvinus, I am ashamed of my authority. This man, my lords, who looks as though he could not hurt a fly, used to chop off heads as easily as a dog sits down. But why should I speak of all those men, and such men? There is no time to lament for public disasters, when one has so many private sorrows to think of. I leave that, therefore, and say only this;

for even if my sister knows no Greek, I do:
The knee is nearer than the shin. This man
you see, who for so many years has been
masquerading under my name, has done
me the favour of murdering two Julias,
great-granddaughters of mine, one by cold
steel and one by starvation; and one great
grandson, L. Silanus. See, Jupiter, whether
in a bad cause (at least it is your own) you
will be fair. Come tell me, blessed Claudius, why of all those you killed, both men
and women, without a hearing, why you did
not hear their side of the case first, before
putting them to death? Where do we find
that custom? It is not done in heaven. Look
at Jupiter: all these years he has been king,
and never did more than once to break Vul-
can's leg,

"Whom seizing by the foot he cast
from the threshold of the sky",

and once he fell in a rage with his wife and
strung her up: did he do any killing? You

killed Messalina, whose great-uncle I was no less than yours. "I don't know", did you say? Curse you! that is just it: not to know was worse than to kill. Caligula he went on persecuting even when he was dead. Caligula murdered his father-in-law, Claudius his son-in-law to boot. Caligula would not have Crassus' son called Great; Claudius gave him his name back, and took away his head. In one family he destroyed Crassus, Magnus, Scribonia, the Tristionias, Assario, noble though they were; Crassus indeed such a fool that he might have been emperor. Is this he you want now to make a god? Look at his body, born under the wrath of heaven! In fine, let him say as many as three words quickly, and he may have me for a slave. God! who will worship this god, who will believe in him? While you make gods of such as he, no one will believe you to be gods. To be brief, my lords: if I have lived honourably among you, if I have never given plain speech to any, avenge my wrongs. This is my motion": then he read out his amendment, which he had committed to writing: "Inasmuch as the blessed Claudius murdered his father-in-law Appius Silanus, his two sons-in-law, Pompeius Magnus and L. Silanus, Crassus Frugi his daughter's father-in-law, as like him as two eggs in a basket, Scribonia his daughter's mother-in-law, his wife Messalina, and others too numerous to mention; I propose that strong measures be taken against him, that he be allowed no delay of process, that immediate sentence of banishment be passed on him, that he be deported from heaven within thirty days, and from Olympus within thirty hours".

This motion was passed without further debate. Not a moment was lost: Mercury screwed his neck and haled him to the lower regions, to that bourne "from which they say no traveller returns". As they passed downwards along the Sacred Way, Mercury asked what was that great concourse of men? could it be Claudius' funeral? It was certainly a most gorgeous spectacle, got up regardless of expense, clear it was that a god was being borne to the grave: tootling of flutes, roaring of horns, an immense brass band of all sorts, such a din that even Claudius could hear it. Joy and rejoicing on every side, the Roman people walking about like free men. Agatho and a few pettifoggers were weeping for grief, and for once in a way they meant it. The Barristers were crawling out of their dark corners, pale and thin, with hardly a breath in their bodies, as though just coming to life again. One of them when he saw the pettifoggers putting their heads together, and lamenting their sad lot, up comes he and says: "Did not I tell you the Saturnalia could not last for ever?"

When Claudius saw his own funeral train, he understood that he was dead. For they were chanting his dirge in anapaests, with much mopping and mouthing:

"Pour forth your laments, your sorrow declare,
Let the sounds of grief rise high in the air:
For he that is dead had a wit most keen,
Was bravest of all that on earth have been.
Racehorses are nothing to his swift feet:
Rebellious Parthians he did defeat;
Swift after the Persians his light shafts go:
For he well knew how to fit arrow to bow,
Swiftly the striped barbarians fled:
With one little wound he shot them dead.
And the Britons beyond in their unknown seas,
Blue-shielded Brigantians too, all these
He chained by the neck as the Romans' slaves.
He spake, and the Ocean with

trembling waves
Accepted the axe of the Roman law.
O weep for the man! This world never saw
One quicker a troublesome suit to decide,
When only one part of the case had been tried,
(He could do it indeed and not hear either side).
Who'll now sit in judgment the whole year round?
Now he that is judge of the shades underground
Once ruler of fivescore cities in Crete,
Must yield to his better and take a back seat.
Mourn, mourn, pettifoggers, ye venal crew,
And you, minor poets, woe, woe is to you!
And you above all, who get rich quick
By the rattle of dice and the three card trick".

Claudius was charmed to hear his own praises sung, and would have stayed longer to see the show. But the Talthybius of the gods laid a hand on him, and led him across the Campus Martius, first wrapping his head up close that no one might know him, until betwixt Tiber and the Subway he went down to the lower regions. His freedman Narcissus had gone down before him by a short cut, ready to welcome his master. Out he comes to meet him, smooth and shining (he had just left the bath), and says he: "What make the gods among mortals?" "Look alive", says Mercury, "go and tell them we are coming". Away he flew, quicker than tongue can tell. It is easy going by that road, all down hill. So although he had a touch of the gout, in a trice they were come to Dis's door. There lay Cerberus, or, as Horace puts it, the hundred-headed monster. Claudius was a trifle perturbed (it was a little white bitch he used to keep for a pet) when he spied this black shag-haired hound, not at all the kind of thing you could wish to meet in the dark. In a loud voice he cried, "Claudius is coming!" All marched before him singing, "The lost is found, O let us rejoice together!" Here were found C. Silius consul elect, Juncus the ex-praetor, Sextus Traulus, M. Helvius, Trogus, Cotta, Vettius Valens, Fabius, Roman Knights whom Narcissus had ordered for execution. In the midst of this chanting company was Mnester the mime, whom Claudius for honour's sake had made shorter by a head. The news was soon blown about that Claudius had come: to Messalina they throng: first his freedmen, Polybius, Myron, Harpocras, Amphaeus, Pheronactus, all sent before him by Claudius that he might not be unattended anywhere; next two prefects, Justus Catonius and Rufrius Pollius; then his friends, Saturninus, Lusius and Pedo Pompeius, and Lupus and Celer Asinius, these of consular rank; last came his brother's daughter, his sister's daughter, sons-in-law, fathers and mothers-in-law, the whole family in fact. In a body they came to meet Claudius; and when Claudius saw them, he exclaimed, "Friends everywhere, on my word! How came you all here?" To this Pedo Pompeius answered, "What, cruel man? How came we here? Who but you sent us, you, the murderer of all the friends that ever you had? To court with you! I'll show you where their lordships sit".

Pedo brings him before the judgement seat of Aeacus, who was holding court under the Lex Cornelia to try cases of murder and assassination. Pedo requests the judge to take the prisoner's name, and produces a summons with this charge: Senators killed, 35; Roman Knights, 221; others as the sands of the sea-shore for multitude. Claudius finds no counsel. At length out steps P. Petronius, an old chum of his, a finished scholar in the Claudian tongue, and claims a remand. Not granted. Pedo Pompeius prosecutes with loud outcry. The counsel for the defence tries to reply; but Aeacus, who is the soul of justice, will not have it. Aeacus hears the case against Claudius, refuses to hear the other side, and passes sentence against him, quoting the line:

"As he did, so be he done by, this is justice undefiled".

A great silence fell. Not a soul but was stupefied at this new way of managing matters; they had never known anything like it before. It was no new thing to Claudius, yet he thought it unfair. There was a long discussion as to the punishment he ought to endure. Some said that Sisyphus had done his job of porterage long enough; Tantalus would be dying of thirst, if he were not relieved; the drag must be put at last on wretched Ixion's wheel. But it was determined not to let off any of the old stagers, lest Claudius should dare to hope for any such relief. It was agreed that some new punishment must be devised: they must devise some new task, something senseless, to suggest some craving without result.

Then Aeacus decreed he should rattle dice
for ever in a box with no bottom. At once
the poor wretch began his fruitless task of
hunting for the dice, which for ever slipped
from his fingers.

"For when he rattled with the box,
and thought he now had got 'em,
The little cubes would vanish thro'
the perforated bottom.
Then he would pick 'em up again, and
once more set a-trying:
The dice but served him the same
trick: away they went a-flying.
So still he tries, and still he fails; still
searching long he lingers;
And every time the tricksy things go
slipping thro' his fingers.
Just so when Sisyphus at last once
gets there with his boulder,
He finds the labour all in vain—it
rolls down off his shoulder".

All on a sudden who should turn up but

Caligula, and claims the man for a slave: brings witnesses, who said they had seen him being flogged, caned, fisticuffed by him. He is handed over to Caligula, and Caligula makes him a present to Aeacus. Aeacus delivers him to his freedman Menander, to be his law-clerk.

ERIS

86–90 Paul Street   265 Riverside Dr. #4G
London EC2A 4NE   New York, NY 10025

English translation by W. H. D. Rouse first pub-
lished in 1913.

The moral rights of the author and translator have
been asserted.

ISBN 978-1-912475-42-1

eris.press